Nattie Parsons'
Good-Luck Lamb

for Becky

♥

Nattie Parsons' Good-Luck Lamb

BY LISA CAMPBELL ERNST

VIKING · KESTREL

Nattie Parsons loved helping her grandfather tend to their small flock of sheep. "Take care," he would caution when Nattie drove the sheep to pasture by herself. "Selling their wool is our only way to make money, and times are hard."

"We'll be just fine," Nattie would reply. "Don't you worry."

Nattie always carried a bag along to collect bits of wool, because the one thing she loved even more than tending the sheep was weaving on her grandfather's loom.

Mr. Parsons had been a weaver, but now his hands were old and stiff. "I'll leave the weaving up to you," he told Nattie. "You sure do have a talent."

At shearing time, there was never enough wool to save a fleece for Nattie's weaving. For now, the scraps she picked up would have to do.

"Someday I'll weave something really pretty," Nattie said wistfully.

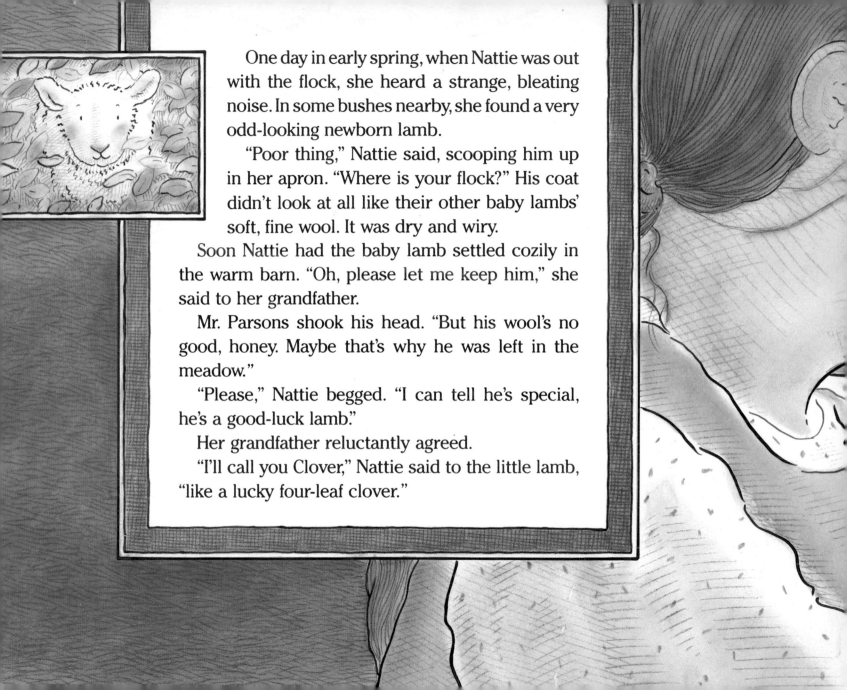

One day in early spring, when Nattie was out with the flock, she heard a strange, bleating noise. In some bushes nearby, she found a very odd-looking newborn lamb.

"Poor thing," Nattie said, scooping him up in her apron. "Where is your flock?" His coat didn't look at all like their other baby lambs' soft, fine wool. It was dry and wiry.

Soon Nattie had the baby lamb settled cozily in the warm barn. "Oh, please let me keep him," she said to her grandfather.

Mr. Parsons shook his head. "But his wool's no good, honey. Maybe that's why he was left in the meadow."

"Please," Nattie begged. "I can tell he's special, he's a good-luck lamb."

Her grandfather reluctantly agreed.

"I'll call you Clover," Nattie said to the little lamb, "like a lucky four-leaf clover."

As Clover grew bigger, his wool grew long and wild. Nattie loved him just the way he was, but sometimes the other lambs made fun of him.

Clover worried about being so different. And whenever Clover worried, he got hungry. Running off across the meadow, he would find a shady spot and nibble on fresh, tender leaves. As time went on, Clover grew round and chubby.

The seasons passed, and Clover lived happily on the little farm with Nattie and her grand-father.

When spring arrived, the other lambs' fleeces were shorn. "Your wool may not be good for selling," Nattie told Clover, "but we should trim it. Otherwise, you'll be hot this summer."

As Clover waited his turn to be shorn, he got so nervous that he ran away to find something to eat. And each time Nattie suggested trimming his coat, Clover disappeared. His coat grew longer and longer.

One Saturday, Nattie and her grandfather rode to town to buy seeds at the dry-goods store.

The store owner was always rude to poor people. "What do you want?" she asked. Nattie handed her a list. "Two packages of carrot seeds. Wait right here." The woman rushed off.

Nattie gazed in wonder at the shelves filled with tempting things. Her eyes stopped near the counter. Displayed there was a pure white shawl more beautifully woven than anything Nattie had imagined.

She walked over and picked up the edge. It was woven in a herringbone pattern, with fancy knots at each corner.

"Don't touch that!" the store owner shouted.

Nattie dropped the shawl. "I-I was just admiring the weaving," she stammered. "I'm a weaver, too."

The woman laughed. "That shawl is made of the finest Tibetan lamb's wool and woven by real artists in Paris, France. It is *very* expensive. You may *think* you're a weaver, my dear, but you could never make something as fine as that."

Over the summer, Nattie and Clover were so happy that they didn't notice how worried Mr. Parsons was. At last he came to Nattie.

"This past year's been a hard one, honey," he said sadly. "There's not enough money to buy hay for the sheep to last the winter. We'll have to sell some of the lambs. We can only keep the ones who have the best wool."

"You wouldn't sell Clover!" Nattie cried. "He won't eat much. He can have my food!"

"I don't have any choice," her grandfather said. "It's our only way to keep the farm going."

That night Nattie lay awake for hours. "There must be another way to make money for hay," she said. "If only I had more wool, I could weave something to sell—like the shawl in the dry-goods store."

She reached down to pat Clover on his head, and her fingers caught in his long, bushy wool. Slowly, a smile came over her face. "It may not be very pretty," she said to herself, "but it's just going to have to do."

"Tomorrow, Clover, we're going to cut your wool. I'll make a beautiful shawl out of it. I'm not sure how, but I'll figure out a way. It's our only chance to save you."

Nattie lay back down, suddenly feeling hopeful. She began to plan every detail of the shawl she would weave.

But now Clover couldn't sleep. All the talk of being sold or shorn had made him begin to worry. The more Clover worried, the hungrier he got.

By dawn Clover was starving and he slipped out to find something to eat. Surely a few bites of something tasty would make him feel better.

At the edge of the meadow, Clover spied an unusual shrub. It was covered—from top to bottom—with big, plump, red berries. Raspberries! Clover gingerly pulled one off and tasted it.

"Baa," he sang. Delicious! The sweet juice dribbled down Clover's chin. "Just a few more," he thought, "and I'll go straight home." But each time Clover decided to stop, he would see another perfect berry too beautiful to pass by. At last he had eaten every one on the bush.

At home Nattie was waiting on the fence, looking for him. "Baaaa!" Clover called. He looked for a smile on Nattie's face as she saw him, but her expression was very different.

"Clover!" she cried. "What has happened to your wool?"

Clover looked to his left, and then his right. He looked up and down. All Clover saw was red.

"You're the color of raspberries!" Nattie said. Clover shook off a leaf and Nattie began to understand. "Your coat was so dry, it must have soaked the juice right up."

She tried not to cry. "Don't worry. We'll just wash it until it's white again, and then we'll make our shawl."

Clover felt very guilty and he stood quite still as Nattie carefully cut off the wiry red wool. But no matter how many times she washed or boiled or rinsed it, the wool stayed the same color.

Finally she gave up. "There's no use," Nattie said, shaking her head, "I'll just have to use it the way it is."

Nattie began the shawl as Clover watched. First, she carded the wool to line up all the strands, then she spun it on her wheel. Nattie pulled and twisted sections evenly to make long pieces of yarn for weaving.

The yarn from Clover's wool was fuzzy and full of lumps. Fibers stuck out in all directions no matter how Nattie fussed with it.

When she began work on the loom, Nattie used her bits of white yarn to make a design.

Row by row, Nattie fell into the rhythm of her weaving. She forgot about being tired. Very slowly, the shawl grew larger.

When Nattie and her grandfather rode into town that Saturday, Nattie held a package wrapped in paper. Clover and the other lambs that Mr. Parsons planned to sell rode in the back.

The store owner frowned when they entered the dry-goods store. "I've come to sell you a shawl," Nattie said in a voice almost too quiet to be heard.

The owner laughed. "Something *you* made? I hardly think it will be suitable for my store!"

Nattie nervously unwrapped the package. Just as she held up the shawl, two customers came in the door.

"My heavens," gasped one, "what a beautiful shawl!"

The other customer took it from Nattie and wrapped it around her shoulders. "It's the finest weaving I have ever seen. And the wool! What marvelous texture and color!" She turned to Nattie. "I must have it, dear, no matter how much it costs."

Nattie smiled.

The money from the shawl was enough to buy hay for the whole winter.

As the cold winds howled outside, and Clover's wool grew back to its usual length, Nattie planned her design for next year's shawl. "Maybe a dovetail weave," she mused, "with set-in embroidery."

"Baaa," Clover answered softly as he dozed by the fire. That was up to Nattie, but he had plans of his own. Clover thought of the patch of wild blueberries that grew at the far end of the meadow. They had always looked tasty.

VIKING KESTREL
Viking Penguin Inc., 40 West 23rd Street, New York, New York 10010, U.S.A.
Penguin Books Ltd, 27 Wrights Lane, London W8 5TZ (Publishing & Editorial) and
Harmondsworth, Middlesex, England (Distribution & Warehouse)
Penguin Books Australia Ltd, Ringwood, Victoria, Australia
Penguin Books Canada Limited, 2801 John Street, Markham, Ontario, Canada L3R 1B4
Penguin Books (N.Z.) Ltd, 182–190 Wairau Road, Auckland 10, New Zealand

Copyright © Lisa Campbell Ernst, 1988
All rights reserved
First published in 1988 by Viking Penguin Inc.
Published simultaneously in Canada
Printed in Hong Kong by Imago Publishing Ltd.
Set in Cheltenham Book
1   2   3   4   5   92   91   90   89   88

Library of Congress Cataloging-in-Publication Data
Ernst, Lisa Campbell.   Nattie Parson's good luck lamb.
Summary: When her grandfather decrees that her cherished lamb
must be sold, Nattie rebels and seeks a way to keep her pet.
[1. Pets—Fiction]   I. Title.   PZ7.E7323Nat
1988   [E]   87-13700   ISBN 0-670-81778-3